WEST VANCOUVER MEMORIAL LIBRARY

D0345030

Withdrawn from Collection

Withdrawn from Collection

WEST VANCOUVER MEMORIAL LIBRARY

WHAT'S IN THE POND?

By Anne Hunter

Houghton Mifflin Company
Boston 1999

Copyright © 1999 by Anne Hunter

All rights reserved. For information about permission
to reproduce selections from this book, write to
Permissions, Houghton Mifflin Company, 215 Park Avenue South,
New York, New York 10003.

The text of this book is set in Goudy.
The illustrations are watercolor, colored pencil, and ink, reproduced in full color.

Library of Congress Cataloging-in-Publication Data

Hunter, Anne.
What's in the pond? / Anne Hunter.
p.   cm.
Summary: Describes a variety of pond animals, including the mayfly, red-winged
blackbird, and painted turtle.
ISBN: 0-395-91224-5
1. Pond animals—Juvenile literature. [1. Pond animals.] I. Title.
QL146.3.H87   1999
591.763'6—dc21   98-46799   CIP   AC

Printed in Singapore
TWP 10 9 8 7 6 5 4 3 2 1

What's in the pond?

A Damselfly

The thin, brightly colored damselfly is a close relative of the dragonfly. The damselfly begins life at the bottom of the pond as a nymph. Reaching adulthood, it takes to the air and lives around the pond on a diet of mosquitoes, aphids, and other small insects. The damselfly is an inch to an inch and a half in length.

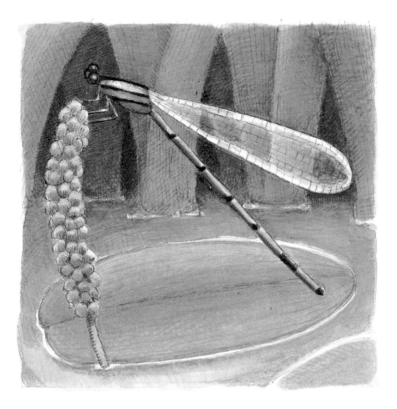

A Bluegill

A bluegill is also known as a sunfish. It lives in the weedy shallows of the pond, feeding on snails and insects. The female lays her eggs in a nest, a round sandy depression in the pond bottom that she makes by fanning away debris with her mouth and tail. An adult bluegill measures from four to ten inches.

A Red-Winged Blackbird

The red-winged blackbird lives and nests in the cattails and rushes of the pond. It eats seeds, insects, and spiders. The streaky brown coloring of the female redwing blends into the color of her nest, making it hard for predators to see her. Red-winged blackbirds are about nine inches long from beak to tail.

A WATER STRIDER

The water strider is an insect that skates on the surface of the pond. Each of its six feet is covered with many tiny hairs that keep the water strider afloat. It feeds on dead insects it finds floating on top of the water. The body of the water strider measures a half inch or so in length.

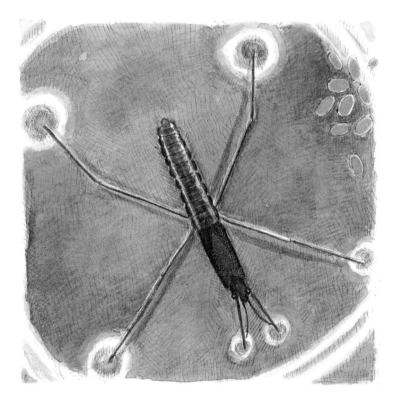

A Chorus Frog

A chorus frog is a type of tree frog. It lives around the edges of the pond. The chorus frog makes a sound like fingernails running over the teeth of a fine-toothed comb. In the spring, chorus frogs all call at once in search of a mate, making a loud chorus of sound. Chorus frogs live on a diet of insects and are about an inch in length.

A Mayfly

The delicate mayfly dances in the air around the pond, balanced by two or three long hairlike tails. The young mayfly, called a nymph, spends its first year or so underwater, feeding on small plants. After developing wings, the mayfly takes to the air, mates, lays its eggs, and dies, all within a few hours. The body of the mayfly measures a quarter to a half inch.

A Large Water Beetle

The large water beetle is probably the fiercest predator in the pond. Although only one to one and a half inches long, the large water beetle is capable of catching prey much larger than itself. It hunts underwater, diving after minnows, tadpoles, and insects, which it captures in its strong jaws.

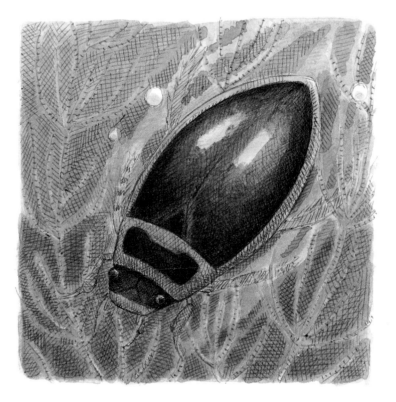

A Painted Turtle

The painted turtle is one of several kinds of basking turtles. Basking turtles are pond dwellers that often pull themselves up onto logs or rocks to bask in the sun. Painted turtles eat frogs, tadpoles, fish, and plants. In cold climates, they hibernate at the bottom of the pond during the winter. An adult painted turtle measures about ten inches long.

BULLFROG TADPOLES

A tadpole is a young frog. The big bullfrog's tadpole is one of the largest tadpoles in the pond. After hatching from an egg, the tadpole grows for a year or two before developing into a fully grown bullfrog. Tadpoles feed on aquatic plants and insect larvae and vary in length from two to four inches.

A Muskrat

The muskrat lives in and around the pond. It has a flat, furless tail designed for swimming. Muskrats have a varied diet of plants, frogs, tadpoles, fish, and clams. In the winter they live in dome-shaped houses built from cattails. A full-grown muskrat is a foot and a half to two feet long from nose to tip of tail.

The pond is a happening place. The creatures chosen for this book are only a very few of the many that live in the pond or come here to drink, eat, find a mate, lay eggs, or spend the night. Many other creatures live at the pond out of sight, too small to be seen with the naked eye, or buried deep in the mud of the pond bottom. Try looking at some pond water through a magnifying glass. Or sit quietly beside the pond and see what you can see.